BURR AND HAMILTON
a drama for voices

BURR AND HAMILTON
a drama for voices

By | Jeff Humphries

Woodcuts by | Betsy Bowen

Published by Philsgood Press
Minneapolis, Minnesota

Contents

If they sometimes behave like actors in a historical drama, that is often how they regarded themselves.

-Joseph J. Ellis, **Founding Brothers**

As the present work nears completion—as I write this—the two hundredth anniversary of the duel between Alexander Hamilton and Aaron Burr has just passed. As this bicentennial approached, a number of historians revisited the event in works both popular and scholarly—Thomas Fleming, Joseph Ellis, and Roger Kennedy, to name a few. This is not a work of history. It takes liberties with form and substance that are not permitted to the professional historian. What does it offer in return that they cannot? I have tried to reduce the story to an absolute minimum of circumstantial detail on the assumption that such pruning, severe and judicious, might cause an organic line to be revealed—this is a principle of Japanese art, and not the only one in play here. It will, of course, be for others to say if this historical minimalism has been successful, whether the essential, stark, brutal shape of the events has been revealed.

To me, this story demands to be cast in such a spare and densely allusive format because it is an American allegory like no other. The troika of Burr, Hamilton and Jefferson is as crucial to understanding the United States as the three great unifiers of Japan, Oda Nobunaga, Toyotomi Hideyoshi, and Tokugawa Ieyasu, are to understanding Japan. Every Japanese schoolchild knows the story of these three men confronted by a bird in a cage that will not sing: "Nobunaga says, 'Kill the bird.' Hideyoshi says, 'Make the bird want to sing.' Ieyasu says, 'Wait.'" The present drama is not as brief, but it is meant to be just as revealing, and almost as dense.

I have called it "A Drama for Voices" for lack of a better term; it might almost be called a narrative poem, a dramatic poem, or a meditation. It combines several forms: some poetry—blank verse of varying line length and a form which I have adapted from traditional Japanese poetry and found congenial—as well as prose. The latter are not unfinished drafts of the former but prosaic moments requiring expression in prose.

I should note that some editors and a few poets have expressed unease with my adaptation of the Japanese tanka prosody—alternating lines of five and seven syllables, ending in two or more lines of seven. Such objections seem ill-conceived, as there is no poetical form native to English except perhaps the old Anglo-Saxon line of four or five "beats" or stresses. All others, including the best known, are imported and adapted. The "iambs" and "trochees" that

we all studied in high school are not English, but Greek in origin; they refer to forms based on the distinction in Greek of long and short syllables. Since this difference does not exist in English, it was replaced by the difference between "accented" and "unaccented" syllables, even though there is in fact an infinite degree of variation in English between these two extremes, and therefore no pure iambic exists, even in the adapted sense. The Japanese form I have used involves far fewer problems in its adaptation, as it relies far less on properties exclusive to the Japanese language and nonexistent in English.

In the events in question, there is a thematic parallel with an old Japanese custom as well, though no such thing is needed to justify the use of a poetic form borrowed from Japanese, any more than a poem in iambics would need to have some thematic resonance with ancient Greece. The code duello, *the code of honor according to which the formal exchange of potentially lethal gunfire is a last, but necessary resort, is interestingly reflected in the Japanese practice of* seppuku *or* hara kiri, *ritual suicide.* Seppuku, *self-disembowelment, was a way for a defeated or otherwise disgraced samurai to make for himself an honorable death. Hamilton and Burr were both disgraced and defeated politicians* and soldiers—*as near to "samurai" as possible on these shores*—*and both sought vindication of their honor in the ritual of the duel. It has often been speculated that Hamilton may have, in some part of himself, wished to die. If this were true, the drama that unfolded between him and Colonel Burr in July 1804 was a kind of displaced* seppuku, seppuku *"by proxy," as it were. The duel only restored Hamilton's reputation in death, and not Burr's, though each thought he had been driven to the most extreme of remedies by exigencies of honor.*

On another thematic point, some readers will be surprised at how Thomas Jefferson comes off in these pages. They should not be; my representation of him reflects recent scholarship. I have enormous respect and admiration for Mr. Jefferson and have tried to treat him very fairly. If we are to allow him his humanity, then we must let him have his faults. He is not, was not, a statue or a saint. For a century and a half, Jefferson got a virtual "free ride" from historians and biographers, and not by accident. He knew that historians love paper, and he left them lots of it, carefully choosing what not to write down, and what to wax eloquent about. He was nothing if not shrewd; shrewder by far, more calculating and manipulative—not only of contemporaries but of posterity as well—than Burr or Hamilton. It has been speculated that he had another advantage: There is evidence that both Burr

and Hamilton were manic-depressive, and that Jefferson was not. In any case, while Jefferson's name does not appear in the title of this work, he is most assuredly the third protagonist. He may not have been physically present at Weehawken on July 11, 1804, but he was very much there nonetheless, a silent third party to the most famous duel in American history.

From thematic concerns to concerns of genre: This is not a "play" in the usual or strict sense. It is not an attempt to imitate the reality we think we inhabit, but rather to narrate the strange landscape of our collective American imagination, a landscape of history swollen or degenerated into dream and myth.

Though "dramatic," this work is not to be performed except in the mind of the reader, like Alfred de Musset's "drame dans un fauteuil" (armchair theater). Anyone attempting to produce it on the stage will assume entire responsibility. In case anyone should elect to try this, I see one major obstacle that would have to be overcome: The transition from each scene to the next must be lightning fast, or the simplicity and starkness will be blurred, even lost. It would make a fine radio play, or a beautiful film, however.

The characters are long dead, and know themselves to be so. They are ghosts, exciting only as wax figures or two-dimensional images graved on the paper we exchange as currency and affix to letters as postage stamps, disembodied voices haunting our archives and our metaphysical and political souls. They are bound to express themselves in a way unlike that of characters in plays by, say, David Mamet or Edward Albee.

If they must be imagined as having faces and bodies, the reader should remember that all look like dead people, _historic_: waxen, pale, powdered, stiff, not only because they are dead, but to accentuate the irreality of the piece, its quality of an opera in which the music is language. In this I have sought to recreate my own experience of Shakespeare or Sophocles, whose archaic language constitutes for us today a kind of weird rhythmical chant, a verbal chamber music, far removed from everyday speech, highly stylized and ritualistic. It is closer to Japanese Noh drama than to contemporary realism.

All of the characters are historical personages, and more than a few of the words spoken by them are taken directly from documents and letters that they wrote. Their original language has been revised as slightly as possible to make it fit with the rest. §

*E*arly on the morning of July 11, 1804, five men crossed the Hudson River *from New York City to a secluded place near Weehawken, New Jersey to enact a ritual of honor and death. One was Alexander Hamilton, former Secretary of the Treasury, another Aaron Burr, Vice-President; there were also their seconds and a medical doctor. The two greeted one another, and then exchanged pistol shots at ten paces, following the code duello. Hamilton took the first shot, the bullet passing just over Burr's head. Burr took aim with care, and fired at his adversary's abdomen. The bullet found its mark in Hamilton's left side and he died the next day; Burr lived to endure exile, old age, and accusations of treason by President Jefferson, under whom he served. He was tried four times and never found guilty.* §

I

This is an imaginary space, but at the same time a very real one. We are in a sparsely furnished room in which there are three identical tables piled with paper, books, an ink stand, quill pens, sealing wax, a candlestick, etc. At each desk sits a thin, short but long-limbed man with large eyes and nose in a small face, receded hairline. They are dressed exactly alike, and look like the same man. Before our eyes, each puts on a gold Venetian mask tied around his head with a black silk ribbon: one in the shape of a crescent moon, one a bird with a long beak, the third a cat.

MOON: Aaron Burr, late, losing candidate
For governor of New York State,
And still for a brief time Vice-President
Of these precariously United
States,

BIRD: I am he, he am I.
It has been my indignity these last four years
To while away the hours and days
In the most absurd office ever
Devised by human calculation,

CAT: An electoral appointment perfectly made
To shroud its most resourceful occupant
With desuetude and impotence.

BIRD: It fell to me by accident
I should have been president.
I received as many electors' votes
As He—you can be sure
The sage of Monticello
Was surprised.

MOON: Still, I am not
The best, but the only
Politician of these times.
The others—even He,
Despite his famous populist rhetoric—
Turn pale at talk of expanding suffrage.

BIRD: They fear democracy's ineptitude, they fear,
             As Hamilton says, a government
             That does "what will *please* not
             What will benefit the people."

CAT: I say the people must be led astutely.
             They should have whatever
             May please them, so long as I may have
             What pleases me.

BIRD: What pleases me
             Is living well, not emolument or even power.
             Oh yes, I know we are embarking upon a new age
             Of bourgeois frugality, in which even great men
             Are expected to eschew extravagance
             And hoard their cash—for what? For crassness.
             I have little interest in money,
             Except for spending it. I spend it
             Quickly, and in large amounts. Public
             Service has reduced me to indebtedness—

CAT: Not penury, indeed, but a rather
             Opulent indebtedness
             Of mansions and servants.

MOON: It has done the same to Hamilton
             And Him. We borrow from each other.

BIRD: I would be president, and my pockets
             Amply filled with every sort of good,

MOON: And power to do good,
             To do such things as put an end
             To slavery, which befouls the fair visage
             Of liberty and belies our principles,

BIRD: And divides us, dangerously North and South,
             Within this frail, as yet untested Union
             Of independent former colonies,
             Republics and commonwealths
             Unwilling to concede the smallest part
             Of independent sovereignty.

MOON:	An end for which Mr. Hamilton And I cooperate, to our political Detriment, as members of the Manumission Society, but on which He Demurs with great Virginian subtlety, Declining in maturity to extend The rights he lyricized in youth To even a dusky paramour—
BIRD:	His wife's half-sister by her father's Similar, African intemperance— A brown concubine who has Born him chattel offspring.
CAT:	He declines to embroil himself In insoluble dilemmas—
BIRD & MOON:	This is not without solution.
JOHN ADAMS:	Do not forget Mr. Hamilton's Lubricious indiscretions, Why, his secretions are so copious He cannot find whores enough To requite them, and sleeps Even with his wife's sister!
BIRD:	Damn you sir, for this intrusion!
ADAMS:	The bastard brat of a Scots peddler Is sanctimonious without morality; He rises from his best friend's wife's bed To go to church on Sunday morning, As Mr. Latrobe so aptly put it!
CAT:	*A man without lust is an empty husk.* Hypocrisy is another thing. Tom would not even canvass When it looked as though I'd beat him In the Congress, said he'd rather not Be president than owe it to Unsavory engagements.

MOON:

Not so; in fact, 'twas I declined
To purchase votes with promises,
Whilst He dealt secretly
In clandestine assurances to enemies
To purchase their support.

CAT:

This life is but a never finished
Negotiation with fate
And human adversaries.

MOON:

He and Hamilton esteem
Reluctantly this wretched constitution, though
Hamilton suspects, correctly, that it will not
Last, while Tom believes it dangerously empowered,
A threat to holy Virginia's sovereignty.
I tell you, I have said so many
Times, it will not last another
Fifty years. Those unwilling
To renounce the enslavement of humans
Will go mad in their corrupted embrace
Of a liberty which is not for all.

BIRD:

Once, I said to Hamilton
What needed to be done. I advised him
To seize the present opportunity
To give a stable government.
Do you know what the idiot replied?
"Seize?" he said, incredulous
As a country maiden, "Seize? This
Could not be done without—guilt."
I, descendant of Puritan clerics,
Dare question whether guilt
Have any place in our new policy.
Believe the grandson of Jonathan
Edwards in such a matter. Guilt
Means nothing to me. I told Hamilton
Then, "Great souls do not trouble
Themselves about small morals."
He replied, "The thing—to seize—
Was never practical from the genius
And situation of the country."

MOON:	This depends upon one's estimate of human
	Passions and the means of influence
	Upon them. My advantage may consist
	In knowing what these are
	And having no reluctance to appeal
	To them. Others place their faith in <u>laws</u>.
	The law, and even the truth, are
	Whatever may be boldly asserted
	And plausibly maintained. At times a man
	Must make a new law to suit
	Circumstance.
CAT:	He
	Calls me "crooked gun," "perverted
	Machine." But let us understand:
	A machine that comprehends
	The desires of others,
	And from these draws
	Its strength. This makes me
	A prophet of popular sovereignty,
	Or idiot rabble, if you prefer.
BIRD:	General Hamilton, meanwhile,
	Describes me as "a profligate voluptuary,
	As true a Cataline as ever met in secret
	Conclave." He has insulted my motives
	And for this will I make orphans of his progeny.
MOON:	Rather to defend my honor
	Or such of it as has survived the calumnies
	Of those two men, the one so bold,
	The other sly unto hypocrisy,
	The one in presidential auspices invisible
	To the eye of justice, but the other,
	Entirely within my sights and vulnerable to challenge.

Removes mask.

Only one of us is Burr.
The others are inventions
Bad dreams that other men
Have about themselves,

Projecting onto me.
I cannot be held responsible.

Tears the bird mask from its wearer.

This is Hamilton.

Does likewise to cat mask.

This your third President,
All they most fear
All the very worst of themselves
Is visible to them in me. §

II

We see the counting house of Nicholas Cruger, a merchant of Nevis, the West Indies. A boy in his mid-teens sits at a stool, hunched over an account book. There is a full-length mirror propped against a wall. The boy stands up from the stool and rubs his eyes, yawns. He takes down a pistol from where it hangs—one of a pair—on the wall, and examines it. We can tell he has done so before.

HAMILTON: | War is the only way for a man to advance quickly.

He moves to face the mirror, takes aim at himself, and pulls the trigger. The hammer makes a loud click. The gun is not loaded. §

III

The College of New Jersey, now Princeton University. A meeting room. The Reverend John Witherspoon, a Presbyterian clergyman, presides, sitting at the head of a rectangular table. There are several other men present, all dressed the same, in black with the bifurcated tab collar of the clergy.

WITHERSPOON:	What of this Hamilton from the West Indies?
PROFESSOR # 1:	He is a bastard.
PROFESSOR # 2:	And a genius, apparently.
PROFESSOR # 3:	His mother is a woman of low morals, his father a dissolute Scotsman from a family of minor noble blood.
PROFESSOR # 1:	Recommended by his tutor and his employer, a Mr. Nicholas Cruger.
PROFESSOR # 2:	One might well inquire as to the nature of Mr. Cruger's keen interest in the boy, whom one of the letters describes as a strikingly comely youth.
PROFESSOR # 1:	Is he Presbyterian?
PROFESSOR # 3:	The boy or Mr. Cruger?
PROFESSOR # 1:	Either. Both.
PROFESSOR # 2:	There is no indication.
WITHERSPOON:	Has he any formal schooling?
PROFESSOR # 1:	None.
PROFESSOR # 2:	Scots blood or no, he could not be admitted without some formal schooling.
WITHERSPOON:	Agreed. At least a year—or two.
PROFESSOR # 1:	King's College in New York might take him right away.

WITHERSPOON:	I will write a letter to that effect. Who else do we have?
PROFESSOR # 1:	No further applicants for admission. There is only the extraordinary scholarly performance of Mr. Burr to be noted.
PROFESSOR # 2:	Truly one of the most gifted students we have ever had here.
WITHERSPOON:	He reflects great credit to his father, who served this great College so well as her President before me, and his grandfather, one of the greatest clergymen New England has seen.
PROFESSOR # 3:	Excellence is in the blood.
ALL:	Aye, indeed, yes. §

IV

H is several years older now, in an attorney's office in New York.

HAMILTON:	I wish there were a war.
OLDER MAN:	Come now, Mr. Hamilton, you have received a splendid education, graduated King's College with every distinction, passed the bar. You must now embark upon the parchment battlefields of the law. A man may win recognition there as well.
HAMILTON:	Caesar did not gain fame for his prowess in shuffling paper.
OLDER MAN:	Caesar? What a comparison. Ah yes, well, we had best leave to Caesar that which is Caesar's and busy ourselves with matters at hand.
HAMILTON:	Matters at hand are without importance.

He picks up a quill pen as though it were a gun, holding it out at arm's length, aiming at a mirror hung on the wall.

OLDER MAN:	Not to the persons involved, I can tell you that, and they pay us well to agree with them, don't they? But you may get your war before too long, my boy; you may indeed get it, if King George continues his oppressions.
HAMILTON:	Then I pray he shall do so.
OLDER MAN:	Yours is a rash prayer. You pray for danger to us all.
HAMILTON:	Only where there is danger are there heroic deeds, only where there are heroic deeds can there be greatness.
OLDER MAN:	And death, and pillage, and misery.
HAMILTON:	And fame.
OLDER MAN:	Fame. There is no more fickle mistress.
HAMILTON:	Nor any more beautiful and succulent. §

HAMILTON:	There is a splendid war in progress, and I am but a scribe in it.
GEO. WASHINGTON:	Mr. Hamilton, your services are indispensable to me, and to all of us. The war could not proceed without orders and directions.
HAMILTON:	Yes sir. Yet it manages to proceed without funds.
WASHINGTON:	No, it cannot. Another reason why I require your eloquence and persistence. There must be more letters to Congress. We must appeal to our friends like Mr. Adams.
HAMILTON:	The Continental Congress is useless, sir, with all respect. And Mr. Adams has shown himself unable to move it.
WASHINGTON:	I am as frustrated as you. We must appeal to Hancock and Robert Morris for more private funds, and see if the Congress will not reimburse its own.
HAMILTON:	It cannot. It lacks the authority.
WASHINGTON:	So we, and it, must appeal to the states. How can Pennsylvania refuse Mr. Morris? Or Massachusetts her Mr. Hancock? And even if they did, that is no reason for you to follow the example of Mr. Burr, so talented and high-born a young man, too impetuous to serve any master but himself—
HAMILTON:	He serves his countrymen in battle, sir, and wins just fame for it.
WASHINGTON:	The rewards of service here may be less dramatic, but they are greater, yes, I assure you, I shall see to that. Mr. Burr made a great mistake in leaving my service. Do not emulate a man whose ambition exceeds his discipline. §

VI

The scene is the Battle of New York. The Americans have been badly beaten and are retreating. General Henry Knox accompanies a regiment of troops under his command which is in danger of imminent capture or destruction. Knox is a very stout man who clings desperately to what remains of his dignity in the circumstances—the men are in a swamp, and the shouts and cannon of the British can be heard close at hand. Suddenly a young officer appears on horseback.

BURR: General Knox, sir, what on earth are you doing? Lead your men to safety, man!

KNOX: I beg your pardon?

BURR: LEAD YOUR MEN TO SAFETY, before it is too late!

KNOX: I would gladly do so were there any route left open to us!

BURR: There is one; I have just traversed it.

KNOX: And who the devil might you be?

BURR: Captain Aaron Burr, at your service.

KNOX: I am *General* Henry Knox, Mr. Burr; I outrank you, and I tell you, there is no escape from our predicament. All roads to safety are blocked.

BURR: Not so, General. With all respect, there is a clear road to safety directly before you, I have seen it myself.

KNOX: You are mistaken, Captain Burr, and you are remarkably insolent.

BURR: There is no time. Proceed in the direction from which I have just come, and you will find a clear passage.

KNOX: Damn you, there is no clear passage which will not deliver us into the arms of the British.

BURR: (*exasperated and out of patience, dismounting from his horse*) Very well then, I will lead your men myself. This way, quickly, not a moment to lose!

The men follow Burr, General Knox cursing, bringing up the rear. §

VII

he scene is Washington's cabinet. A round table in the center around which are seated: President George Washington; at his left, the Secretary of State; at his right, Alexander Hamilton, Secretary of the Treasury; Edmund Randolph, Attorney General, and Henry Knox, Secretary of War.

WASHINGTON:	Gentlemen, Mr. Hamilton has two proposals he wishes to submit to your considered perusal. I have examined them and am convinced of their merit.
HAMILTON:	Mr. President, my colleagues, there is no more urgent task before this government than to assure the financial stability of the new nation. To that end, the federal government must assume, and promptly pay, the debts incurred by the states during the late war of independence. In so doing, we will relieve the states of a heavy pecuniary burden, and immediately demonstrate to other, elder nations—trading partners—that it is safe and profitable to invest in the United States. Moreover, to achieve a consistent national—federal— financial policy, to ensure the free flow of capital throughout the federal union, we must have a national bank.
HE:	On the model of the Bank of England, I suppose?
HAMILTON:	Just so. France has long suffered the lack of such an institution and would have one now were it not in the grip of anarchy.
HE:	Necessary progress may entail momentary anarchy—
HAMILTON:	And the murder of innocents?
HE:	I do not think that description is warranted, despots are not innocent, but some innocent blood may be spilled to serve the greater good of justice—
HAMILTON:	To quench the bloodlust of an ignorant mob.

WASHINGTON:	Please, Mr. Hamilton, is such language necessary? It distresses me to see you two gentlemen, of whom I am equally fond and esteem so highly, exchanging harsh words.
HAMILTON:	I beg your pardon and that of my colleagues—
RANDOLPH:	Not necessary. I quite agree on the subject of France.
KNOX:	As do I, sir.
HAMILTON:	I thank you, gentlemen, but the President is right. This is not the matter at hand.
HE:	If I may, for the record, France is merely experiencing violence in proportion to the injustice and depravity which have accrued in centuries of monarchic rule.
HAMILTON:	Depravity? How dare anyone from Virginia—or any southern state—accuse others of depravity when you obstruct all efforts to halt the spread of slavery—despite what you yourself wrote against in your draft of the Declaration of Independence!—Your plantations are the very ganglion of depravity, sir, with enslaved concubinage as rampant as it ever was in ancient Barbary.
WASHINGTON:	That will be enough, Mr. Hamilton. You forget I am a Virginian too.
HAMILTON:	But sir, I happen to know that you feel as I do on the subject of slavery!
WASHINGTON:	I recognize the incompatibility of the institution with the principles of our new nation, but I still own slaves. I have not resolved the contradiction to my satisfaction.
HAMILTON:	There are those among us who would leave it unresolved —to our common ruin.
WASHINGTON:	Enough. This discussion is out of order. Return to the matters at hand or I shall adjourn.

HE:	On the matter at hand, what of the states which have already paid their war debts? Will this not impose a new burden on them, through federal taxation to pay the debts of others?
HAMILTON:	The benefit of acting in unison, rather than as a confederacy of individual debtor states, would accrue equally to all.
HE:	My objection stands.
HAMILTON:	Sir, I apologize for my strong words of a moment past. The matter of war debts cannot be parceled out to individual states or confined within the borders of any state or commonwealth; these debts were incurred for the good of all and must now be resolved by all acting as one, or else the world will see that this federal union of ours retains the same weakness as the confederation of states which preceded it.
He:	I supported the new constitution, Mr. Hamilton, only because it contained provisions which ensured respect for the sovereignty of each state within the federal union. What you propose—both the assumption of debt, and the creation of a national bank—exceeds the powers of this government as stated in the Constitution, and usurps powers which properly reside with the states. I cannot support your proposals.
WASHINGTON:	Mr. Randolph, Mr. Knox, what say you?
RANDOLPH:	I am sensitive to the concerns of my colleague and fellow Virginian, but also to the arguments of Mr. Hamilton. Since these matters fall within the purview of the Department of the Treasury, rather than of State, I am inclined to defer to Mr. Hamilton's wishes.
WASHINGTON:	Mr. Knox?
	Knox has dozed off. Hamilton drops a large book on the floor to wake him.

WASHINGTON:	Mr. Knox, What say you?
KNOX:	What? What say I?
WASHINGTON:	On the matter of Mr. Hamilton's proposals?
KNOX:	Mr. Hamilton's proposals . . .
WASHINGTON:	Regarding the establishment of a national bank, and the assumption of the war debts of the states by the federal government?
KNOX:	Oh yes, well, on these matters, I am not qualified to judge, and therefore, defer to the wisdom of my colleagues.
HE:	If I may, gentlemen, these proposals will serve no one so well as those financial speculators and opportunists —many of them in New York City and Philadelphia, as well as abroad—who have purchased the obligations of the states at a heavy discount from veterans of the late war. The money ought to go to the latter, not the former.
HAMILTON:	The funds must go to those who hold the notes. It is not for us to nullify the right of any individual to sell a financial instrument if he chooses to do so without coercion from any quarter.
HE:	What of the coercion of need? Of poverty?
HAMILTON:	Nothing will subject as many to poverty as not placing the financial affairs of this nation on a solid ground of collective solvency.
HE:	Let the record show, Mr. President, that once again, the Secretary of State begs to dissent. §

VIII

The scene is a tavern. Two unidentified members of Congress converse over ale and pipes.

CONGRESSMAN 1:   Did you hear the news from Albany? The great little Hamilton's father-in-law, the invincible General Philip Schuyler, has been defeated for re-election to the Senate.

CONGRESSMAN 2:   No! I don't believe it! How could it happen?

CONGRESSMAN 1:   It could happen because Hamilton is an arrogant, conceited bastard, and General Schuyler a pompous bore who believes himself entitled to power by birth.

CONGRESSMAN 2:   Good lord. By whom defeated?

CONGRESSMAN 1:   Aaron Burr. Charming, brilliant, no one could say a thing against him.

CONGRESSMAN 2:   I have heard it said he cuts a wide swath through the fairer sex, to the point of licentiousness—

CONGRESSMAN 1:   A trait he shares with Hamilton—let us hope the only one! §

IX

We are in a private room in a tavern somewhere. Present are Senator Gouverneur Morris of New York, newly appointed Chief Justice John Marshall, Congressman Theodore Sedgewick of Massachusetts, Congressman James Bayard of Delaware, and Alexander Hamilton.

MORRIS:	It is still firmly deadlocked: seventy electoral votes apiece for Long Tom and Burr, only sixty-five for Adams.
MARSHALL:	And General Pinckney—bless him—bringing up the rear.
MORRIS:	Many Federalists fear Him far more than Burr; the latter is a gentleman of Northern taste and manners, the scion of fine New England Puritan stock, and he is a practical man, not a radical Jacobin.
MARSHALL:	A practical man indeed, and a *soldier* of proven mettle. Let us not forget the Sage's disappearance after writing the Declaration—
MORRIS:	And His ignominious abandonment, as wartime governor, of the capital of his beloved Virginia to British occupation and pillage.
MARSHALL:	He fled in the middle of the night, half-dressed, on horseback, incognito, trembling with fear like an old woman, and was nearly impeached for it by the legislature.
MORRIS:	So much for His grand words of defiance—cowards become tyrants when they are given power.
MARSHALL:	He is my cousin, I know Him. The first thing He would do is attack the independence of the national judiciary.
HAMILTON:	No, I have known Him more recently; He has pretensions to character; as to Burr, there is nothing in his favor. His private character is not defended by his most impartial friends. If he can, he will certainly

	disturb our Institutions to secure *permanent power* to himself, and with it wealth. He is the Catiline of America, and has no principle, public or private.
MORRIS:	But with such a man we might negotiate.
HAMILTON:	He could be bound by no agreement, and will listen to no monitor but his own ambition; he is sanguine enough to hope every thing, daring enough to attempt every thing, wicked enough to scruple nothing.
MARSHALL:	Perhaps, but to The Red Fox I have insuperable objections. His sympathies with the French in their present state of despotic anarchy would do us great harm in foreign matters, while He would embody himself with the House of Representatives and impose on us the tyranny of pure Democracy, a blow from which the presidency would never recover.
HAMILTON:	He is not without integrity; in His thoughts, at least, He is noble. Mr. Burr has thoughts for nothing but himself. The Federalists should negotiate with Mr. Secretary of State.
MARSHALL:	Believing that you know Burr well, and are impartial, my preference would not be for Burr, but if that is the case, I can take no part in this business. I cannot bring myself to aid my cousin.
SEDGEWICK:	Among our party, the disposition to prefer Mr. Burr has increased until it is nearly unanimous.
HAMILTON:	If the Federalists adopt Burr, I am no more a Federalist. I am obliged to repudiate any party that would so degrade itself and the nation.
BAYARD:	With all respect, I think them both degenerates, and Mr. Burr is proven not to be the practical man we thought he was. There are three of us in three key states prepared to switch to Burr and make him President, with only certain assurances from him—

MARSHALL:	That he will leave the judiciary alone—
BAYARD:	That among them, yes—and he will not even speak to them.
SEDGEWICK:	He neither accepts nor rejects our overtures, choosing silence as his messenger.
HAMILTON:	Perhaps it may be different with Him. He will not deal directly, however. Approach His friends, Messrs Madison and Monroe, or *their* friends—General Smith of Maryland, or Congressman John Nicholas of Virginia —would be my suggestion. §

X

For thirty-five ballots, Burr and *The Moonshine Philosopher of Monticello* each received an equal number of votes in the House of Representatives. On the thirty-sixth ballot, the latter was chosen by ten states to six for Burr. Two federalist-controlled states, South Carolina and Delaware, cast strategic blank votes, and the federalist members of two other states' delegations, those of Maryland and Vermont, absented themselves or abstained to allow their states to go to Him. §

XI

The newly elected President's study. He is a tall, craggy man; His dress is slightly unkempt, and He wears slippers on His feet. His face and gestures reveal nothing of His thoughts. Vice-President Burr, the only other person present, is elegantly dressed. The President's distaste for His visitor is only barely concealed; Burr does not appear to reciprocate it and on the contrary may seem actually perplexed by it.

BURR: Mr. President, I thank you for the favor of this meeting on somewhat short notice.

The President nods.

BURR: *(continuing)*
It has become clear—though You have never said so—that Your choice for a vice-presidential candidate in the next election will not be the same as it was in the last—that is to say, I shall be retiring from the office.

He says nothing and is expressionless.

BURR: This being the case, I have decided, at the urging of many friends, to stand for election to the governorship of New York state.

Burr pauses, awaiting a reaction, which does not come.

BURR: *(continuing)*
I ask only one thing of You in this matter. Not an endorsement, certainly, but Your commitment as a gentleman not to become involved in the election in any way, on any side.

HE: Mr. Burr, I shall be pleased to honor this request.

BURR: I have Your word then?

He nods.

Burr departs.

The President is joined by Madison and Monroe.

HE: He has confirmed that he will stand for election to the governorship of New York.

MADISON: It is no surprise to anyone.

HE: It must not be allowed to happen. All our friends in New York—Governor Clinton, his nephew the mayor and all their friends, and most particularly the journalists we employ, Mr. Callender first—must be marshaled against the possibility of his election. Burr is never to be underestimated. We made the mistake of doing so once; it must not be repeated. He has friends among the Federalists; he and Governor Jay are quite united on the issue of slavery, and have a long history of cooperation on the issue—meaning that they would not hesitate to usurp the right of the states to decide the issue for themselves.

MONROE: I suspect that we may have a prominent Federalist on our side in the matter. Mr. Hamilton—or as he styles himself now, General Hamilton—

MADISON: In emulation of General Bonaparte!

Laughter.

MONROE: Indeed—he may, I believe, be relied on to oppose Burr with all his might.

MADISON: But I thought they were friends, of a sort. Was it not Burr who mediated the dispute between You and Hamilton—

HE: When it was about to manifest as a duel.

MONROE: Yes, that is true, but their friendship is one of rivals, ever on the verge of hatred.

MADISON: But since the defeat of his father-in-law for re-election to the Senate—

MONROE: By none other than Burr—

MADISON: Precisely—and the failure of his plot to elect Pinckney
               president instead of Adams—

MONROE: And of every other plot he has tried to launch—

MADISON: *(grinning)*
               Except the one by which he claims to have defeated
               Burr's designs on the presidency—

HE: Which, though I do not credit as decisive or even of
               much influence, were most welcome—

MADISON: In the wake of all these events, and the death of his great
               and only sponsor, Washington, Hamilton's political
               influence has been reduced to a narrow circle.

HE: All the more reason to rely on our own resources.

MADISON: Yes, but his political weakness will sting Hamilton into
               a frenzy against his rival. And with any luck, they may
               exhaust their venom upon each other, leaving them none
               to expend upon us. §

XII

L ewis's Tavern in Albany, New York; the Federalist Party caucus to decide the party's candidate for governor.

HAMILTON: It has been suggested that the party ought better to support Mr. Burr than put forth its own candidate, and risk the election of our opponents by splitting their opposition. Mr. Burr puts himself forth in the present instance as an independent, and his divorce from the President and the Democratic Party is public knowledge. He has legitimate claim, it is true, to having acted often in affinity with Federalist principle, however, gentlemen, know this without question: Burr does nothing for principle, and all in calculation of his own best interest. He cannot with justice be said less radical than the President, if we take "radical" in its proper sense, to denote extremity of purpose and deficiency of restraint. Friends, there is no more debauched, debased, and corrupt a soul presently at large in this nation than Mr. Burr.

FEDERALIST 1: He is so described even in *The American Gazette*, the paper of Mr. Cheetam, his friend—

FEDERALIST 2: Mr. Cheetam is the Presidential mouthpiece!

HAMILTON: It was Burr who helped Cheetam to buy the paper in question—

FEDERALIST 2: With respect, General Hamilton, their estrangement since that time is known.

FEDERALIST 2: For all we know, there may be good cause for it.

HAMILTON: Evil estranges all, once revealed.

FEDERALIST 1: It cannot be denied that Burr's character is questioned by many without reason to despise him, including General Hamilton.

FEDERALIST 2:	He is widely resented for his success, and hated for his amiability by those who lack it.
FEDERALIST 3:	Enough! If the party cannot speak as one, let every man go his own way. General Hamilton's words should weigh heavily on us all. §

XIII

The President's office.

SENATOR JAMES MONROE:	Hamilton's denouncement of the Vice President has been made public in the New York press. Burr is opposed by all Federalists loyal to Hamilton and all Democrats loyal to us. He cannot win.
HE:	It is done then. He is ruined.
MONROE:	While he has breath, he is not ruined. But he will not be elected governor of New York State. §

XIV

Burr to Hamilton, following the election:

It has been stated
In the press that you defamed
My person in ways
Calculated to affect
The late election.
I demand satisfaction.
Assure me you did
Not, apologize, or meet
Me as a brother-soldier.

Hamilton to Burr in reply:

I cannot comply
Without some more specific
Summary of what
I am supposed to have said
Which has given you offense.

BURR:

I find your answer does not
Satisfy my late request. §

XV

The scene is a ledge approximately six feet wide by forty feet long, twenty feet or so above the Hudson river on the New Jersey Palisade, a mile and a half from the little town of Weehawken. Hoboken, to the south, does yet exist. The ledge is accessible from the shore of the river only at low tide. It is early morning, about seven o'clock, Wednesday, July 11, 1804. There is a thick mist. First two men—Aaron Burr and his second, William P. Van Ness—appear. They remove their coats and set about clearing the space of fallen branches and debris. Three more men appear: Dr. David Hosack, with his medical bag, Nathaniel Pendleton, carrying a case of pistols, and Alexander Hamilton. The two parties greet each other somberly and silently. Van Ness and Pendleton confer briefly over the rules to be observed, and nod agreement, while the principals stand some distance away on either side.

PENDLETON: Dr. Hosack will stand aside
With his back to us,
so that he shall see nothing.
General Hamilton, having been challenged,
Has chosen the weapons.

Pendleton proffers the open case to Van Ness, who removes one.

VAN NESS: They are his brother-in-law, Mr. Church's,
Are they not? According to the rules of honor, their
Barrels are shorter than eleven inches,
And smooth within. They will be loaded
With .54 caliber smooth balls.
We have brought our own.
Mr. Pendleton and I shall throw a coin
To decide the choice of positions,
And who shall give the signal to fire.
Mr. Pendleton, you may call the toss.

PENDLETON: Heads.

VAN NESS: *(having tossed the coin)*
The choice of position is yours.

Pendleton examines the light in both directions, whispers to Hamilton, who nods agreement.

PENDLETON:	General Hamilton has chosen The position facing the river, with his back to the cliff.
BURR:	*(muttering)* Good Lord, sir why? The sun will Be in his eyes.
VAN NESS:	Now I shall toss the coin again To determine which of us Shall give the signal. You may choose.
PENDLETON:	Heads again.
VAN NESS:	You have won again.
PENDLETON:	Gentlemen, you will stand separated By a distance of ten paces, marked by Mr. Van Ness. I will inquire of both of you if you are ready. When you both shall have said yes, I will call out to you: "Present," At which time you may fire at will. Now we will load the pistols.

The two parties withdraw to opposite sides.

PENDLETON:	*(softly)* Shall I set the hair trigger?
HAMILTON:	Not this time.

Hamilton and Burr walk to their positions and assume the prescribed pose: right foot two feet in front of the left, head squared over right shoulder, presenting the smallest possible target.

PENDLETON:	Are you both ready?
HAMILTON:	A moment, please, I am not ready.

He removes spectacles from a pocket with his left hand, puts them on, adjusts them, raises his pistol several times in various directions, squinting down the barrel.

HAMILTON:	Ready.
PENDLETON:	Are you ready Colonel Burr?
BURR:	I am, sir.
PENDLETON:	Very well then—*Present!*

Hamilton raises the pistol above his head, brings it down, and fires. The bullet passes over Burr's head.
Burr raises his pistol, takes aim, and fires. Hamilton falls. Hosack turns and rushes to him. Burr moves to go to Hamilton, but is prevented by Van Ness.

HOSACK:

The bullet has entered his body
Four inches above the right hip,
Making a hole two inches in diameter.
It has struck a rib, gone through the liver,
And lodged in the lumbar vertebra
Which is shattered.

HAMILTON:

It is a mortal wound, Doctor.
Take care of that pistol sir, it is cocked
And not discharged; it may do harm.

HOSACK:

Do not try to move or speak, please.

HAMILTON:

Pendleton knows
I was resolved not to fire at him.
In the first round.

BURR:

I would speak to him.

VAN NESS:

(shielding Burr with a black cloak)
No, sir, we must go.

Burr and Van Ness leave the scene, Burr stopping and turning once to look back. §

XVI

Hamilton is borne into the home of William Bayard, a friend. Dr. Hosack administers laudanum for pain. The ball has pierced the second or third false rib, passing through the liver and the diaphragm, and come to rest at the second lumbar vertebra, which it shattered. No feeling remains in the lower extremities. The French consul, General Rey, sends a surgeon from a French frigate anchored in the harbor, a man expert in the treatment of such wounds, and Hamilton is examined by Dr. Post, of Columbia's medical faculty. All agree they can do nothing. Bishop Moore is sent for to administer the Episcopal communion. He can still speak.

HAMILTON:	My dear Bishop Moore, you must perceive my circumstances. I am aware you disapprove of the evil custom I have fallen to. But do not let me die without the succor of the church.
BISHOP MOORE:	Very well. But if you should regain your health, will you never be engaged in a similar transaction? And will you promise to wield all influence in society to discountenance this barbarous custom?
HAMILTON:	That, sir, is my deliberate intention.
BISHOP MOORE:	Are you disposed to live in love and charity with all men?
HAMILTON:	I harbor no grudge against Colonel Burr. I met him resolved to do him no harm. I forgive all that has happened.
BISHOP MOORE:	*(beginning to administer the communion)* The Body of our Lord Jesus Christ, which was given for thee, preserve thy body and soul unto everlasting life . . .

Alexander Hamilton died at two in the afternoon on the following day. He was interred on July the fourteenth at Trinity Church. In the funeral procession, his grey horse, bedecked with black accoutrements, was led by two black servants, with his empty boots reversed in the stirrups. All along the route was lined with people. In the harbor,

all flags stood half-masted. British frigates and French fired guns in salute for forty-eight minutes, and were hung with black. Gouverneur Morris, stylist of the Constitution, gave the funerary oration.

On the coffin are placed a sword and general's hat. Gouverneur Morris, an imposing, corpulent man of late middle-age, and with one elegantly turned and polished wooden leg, stands next to the coffin.

GOUVERNEUR
MORRIS:

Far from attempting to excite your emotions, I must try to repress my own, and yet I fear that instead of words befitting a public speaker, you shall hear the lamentations of a wailing friend. Remember this solemn testimonial: He was not ambitious. He was ambitious only of glory. I charge you to protect his fame. It is all he has left—all that these poor orphan children will inherit from their father. I charge you to protect his fame. Let it be the test by which you examine all who seek your favor. Disregarding professions, view their conduct, and on doubtful occasions ask, would Hamilton have done this thing? I cannot, must not dwell. It might excite emotions stronger than our better judgement. §

XVII

Vice-President Burr returns to Richmond Hill, his home, the day of the duel, and goes about his usual affairs, receiving reports from friends and servants—which surprise him—of the public anger and sorrow at news of the duel's outcome. He is advised to stay away from his office in the City.

When indicted for murder in New York and New Jersey, he flees to Pennsylvania, and resumes his duties as President of the Senate some months later. His political career is over, however. By killing Hamilton, he had, as Congressman John Randolph of Virginia put it, "fallen like Lucifer, never to rise."

He is rumored to be involved in a plot to establish a new republic comprising parts of New Spain and the western states and territories. Put on trial for treason, he is found innocent on four occasions and exiles himself to Europe, where he becomes addicted to laudanum and opium, and nearly starves. He is rescued from this fate by the friendship and generosity of several prominent Europeans, including the British philosopher Jeremy Bentham, and returns to the United States and to New York City in June 1811, where he resumes the practice of law and lives to "a green old age." §

XVIII

e are at the palisades above the Hudson River, on the New Jersey side at Weekawken. Burr is old now, wears glasses, and walks with a cane. He is in the company of a younger man.

BURR:

Is it twenty-five

Years since we stood here? Nothing

Would seem to have changed,

Except me. I was

What people my age call young,

But time is a strange

Trick: one sees a different

Person looking back

From the very same mirror.

And here we both stand

Turned to stones, fixed in waxen

Staring effigies,

While Time's dumb stepchild, History,

Intones forever,

"Aaron Burr what hast thou done?

"Though hast shot great Hamilton!"

It was I who made him great,

You idiots, can you not see?

Hamilton stood there,

By his own choice, with the sun

Rising in his eyes;

I never knew why,

Unless it was because he

Wanted to be sure

I had a clear view of him.

I do not regret

I killed him; he deserved it

But I knew then

He had not cost me

The election; no one cared

What Hamilton said

In politics by that time;

It was He,

Who had manipulated

Everything, as always,

While remaining distant.

It was a matter

Of honor, which Hamilton

Understood as I

But He did

Not—He, who wrote as famous

A pledge of honor

As exists—Him, honor could

Not bind. The entire

Conundrum of a nation

Is told in this fact:

That He,

Who never freed His

Slaves, wrote the greatest

Document ever written

Against tyranny.

My greatest error

Was not to take the office

Of the president

Away from Him while it lay

Within my own grasp.

Once Hamilton had fallen,

The duel began

With The Noble Agrarian, a duel

Of words, in which He

Never spoke one to my face.

He encrypted me

In lies—though it is true I

Had been asked to be

First president of a new

Republic in the West, I

Never said I would

And I never broke the law.

If treasonous thoughts

Are treason before the law,

There were then traitors

At large in great multitudes.

Four times He had me

Put on trial; four times I was

Declared not guilty.

Had I not fled to Europe

There would have been no ending

To it even then...

I was guilty of nothing

But influence, ease

In public—something which He

Sorely lacked—and some

Measure of success for which

I owed Him nothing.

It was not that I opposed

Him, but that I might

Have done so had I chosen.

And that I had almost been

President instead of Him.

For that I am convicted

At the bar of history.

It would be truer to say:

Aaron Burr, what hast thou done?

Thou hast exceeded Jefferson,

But the truth is manifold,

And the public care nothing

For any but simple truths. §

XIX

September 1836, Burr's deathbed in his room at the Hotel Saint James at Port Richmond, Staten Island, where he spent his final years. He is attended by a Congregationalist minister, Mr. Van Pelt.

VAN PELT:

Do you repent you
Of your sins, offer your soul
To your saviour,
And declare your allegiance
To the faith of your forebears?

BURR:

On that subject, I am coy. §

JEFF HUMPHRIES lives and writes in New Orleans. He is the author of several books, including *A Bestiary,* a collection of poems. His fiction has been published in the Best American Short Stories series, and he is the recipient of an American Academy of Poets award.

BETSY BOWEN, an award-winning artist, makes woodblock prints on the north shore of Lake Superior in Grand Marais, Minnesota, where she operates Betsy Bowen Studio, a fine art family print shop. She is the author and illustrator of *Antler, Bear, Canoe: A Northwoods Alphabet Year.*

Also by Jeff Humphries and illustrated by Betsy Bowen: *Borealis*, a collection of poems, University of Minnesota Press.